the Last Day of School

For Cat Bowman Smith
—L. B.

For Ian Lauri,
who makes life so interesting
—A. G.

With a thousand thanks to Ann Quinn and the students in Dublin City Schools

Margaret K. McElderry Books • An imprint of Simon & Schuster Children's Publishing Division • 1230 Avenue of the Americas, New York, New York 10020 • Text copyright © 2006 by Louise Borden • Illustrations copyright © 2006 by Adam Gustavson • All rights reserved, including the right of reproduction in whole or in part in any form. • Book design by Sonia Chaghatzbanian • The text for this book is set in Carré Noir. • The illustrations for this book are rendered in oil. • Manufactured in China • 10 9 8 7 6 5 4 3 2 1 • Library of Congress Cataloging-in-Publication Data • Borden, Louise. • The last day of school / Louise Borden ; illustrated by Adam Gustavson.—1st ed. • p. cm. • Summary: Matthew Perez, the official timekeeper of Mrs. Mallory's third grade class, has a special good-bye gift for her. • ISBN-13: 978-0-689-86869-6 ISBN-10: 0-689-86869-3 (hardcover) • [1. Teachers—Fiction. 2. Schools—Fiction. 3. Gifts—Fiction.] I. Gustavson, Adam, ill. II. Title. PZ7.B64829Las 2005 • [Fic]—dc22 • 2003025124

FIRST
EDITION

the Last Day of School

written by **louise borden** + illustrated by **adam gustavson**

MARGARET K. MCELDERRY BOOKS
New York London Toronto Sydney

During the last week of May,
the big countdown began.
There were only ten days left
on the Albert E. Chapman Elementary School calendar.

Then there were

nine . . .

eight . . .

seven . . .

six . . .

five . . .

four . . .

three . . .

two . . .

Finally!
June 4th!

It was the last day of school
for the Chapman students and staff,
including Mrs. Mallory's third graders.

Thank you, terrific students!
What an A+ year!

That morning,
Mrs. Mallory wrote her last daily message of the year
neatly in chalk on the blackboard in Room 6,
just as the line of yellow buses
rumbled up the school driveway at 8:20 A.M.
and began to unload the students
one by one.

Room 6 had tall windows that let in the sunlight,
shiny wooden floors that creaked,
a cage with a hamster named Rhoda,
and twenty-three desks for the students
whom Mrs. Mallory had taught all year.

It was a classroom full of books
by Mrs. Mallory's favorite authors,
and other important things
that third graders use—
like graphs and maps and computers
and folders and *more* folders.

On the wall above the teacher's desk
was a round-faced clock with two black hands
that scratched the minutes by,
tick tick,
and *never* seemed to keep the right time.

"I love teaching these students.
We learn from each other,
so we're double trouble in here,"
Mrs. Mallory always joked each September
on Parent Information Night.

But like every school year,
this one had somehow zoomed by.
Papers and projects had been taken home,
and books and school supplies had been put away
during the countdown days
and were stacked neatly on Mrs. Mallory's shelves
for the coming summer months.

Now,
on this morning of June 4th,
519 Chapman students,
from wiggly kindergartners to cool fifth graders,
crowded through the front doors
and hurried down the hallways to their classrooms
for the very last time this school year.

Everyone was talking in extra-loud voices
about the special picnic at lunchtime—
"Fifth graders only!" . . .

about the giant lollipops that Mrs. Graf,
the school secretary,
was handing out to the kids
who had had perfect attendance . . .

about the longer recess
scheduled for all grades . . .

about the snazzy, jazzy music
that Mr. Frazier, the principal,
was playing over the P.A. system . . .

and about the farewell gifts
some of the students had in their backpacks
to give to their teachers.

Matthew Perez listened to the Chapman students
he passed in the hallways
on his way to Room 6.
He peeked in his backpack
to check the package tied with ribbon
and then smiled to himself
as he walked into his classroom
on his last day as a third grader.
Mrs. Mallory was going to *love* his good-bye gift.

Matt loved sports,
and he was as quick as lightning
in the football games during recess.
When the principal joined in and played quarterback,
Matt was a whiz at catching Mr. Frazier's passes,
dodging his classmates,
and running with the ball for a touchdown.

Matt was also good at numbers and time.
Every day he wore a blue Chicago Cubs wristwatch to school.
Matt always knew the correct time,
down to the exact minute and second.

For the past year
Mrs. Mallory had assigned Matt a special job of his own:
"Official Timekeeper of Room 6."
Several times during the school day,
Matt quietly checked his Cubs watch
and then stepped up onto Mrs. Mallory's desk chair
and stood on his tiptoes
to reset the hands on the classroom clock
to the correct time.

Matt knew to the minute when recess was about to begin.
He knew when it was time for his class
to go to Gym and Music and Library and Art,
and he knew when the lunch bell was about to buzz loudly
throughout Chapman Elementary School.

During the countdown days,
Mrs. Mallory and her class
had attended to important final details
before the end of the school year.
Overdue library books were found
and returned.
Desks were cleaned out and scrubbed.
Students rummaged through the Lost and Found.

On each busy day,
the minutes ticked by on the wall clock,
which Matt carefully monitored
with his Cubs watch.
More than once
Mrs. Mallory walked past Matt's desk,
shook her head,
and sighed.
"How will my class ever stay on schedule next year
without our *terrific* timekeeper?"

Near the teacher's overflowing desk
a to-do list was pinned on the wall
and checked off,
task by task.
Plants were given away.
Posters were rolled up.

Then Mrs. Mallory held a special
"Vacation Home for Rhoda" raffle
because everyone had offered to keep
the popular hamster over the summer.

RHODA RAFFLE

Now,
on the morning of June 4th,
Mrs. Mallory stood in the doorway of Room 6
and greeted her students.
She waved to a group of second graders
who were headed down the hall to their classroom.
Some of them hoped
she would be their teacher next fall,
but they wouldn't know
until they opened their report cards,
signed by Mr. Frazier,
at the end of the day.

Today Mrs. Mallory would be saying good-bye
to each of her third graders.
Next fall they would be moving on to fourth grade
and to other Chapman teachers.
She would miss these kids.
After a wonderful year as their teacher,
Mrs. Mallory knew her students
like a mother hen knows her chicks.

June 4th at Chapman Elementary School
was *indeed* a day to remember.

Some classes wrote funny Last Day poems.
The first graders made Last Day hats
and wore them in a spur-of-the-moment parade.
The departing fifth graders gave Mr. Fields,
the custodian,
a special key ring with his name on it.
The art teacher brought in paintbrush cookies
for her Last Day classes.
Mrs. Bell, the gym teacher,
  wore a T-shirt that said SUMMER!
            The school cooks put on chef hats
                and sang to students in the cafeteria line.

And the second graders made AWESOME YEAR! badges
for the bus drivers.

The last day was an ending and a beginning
all mixed up together,
a day when most of the Chapman teachers
looked a bit *frazzled* from the busy weeks in May.
Mr. Frazier e-mailed hastily to the staff:
"We're almost to the finish line!"

In Room 6
everyone swapped lists of favorite books
for summer reading.
Then students began to whisper among themselves,
and slowly,
shyly,
one by one,
they presented Mrs. Mallory
with her good-bye cards and presents.
Matt stood at the edge of the group
crowded around his teacher's desk.
He craned his neck for a better look
and watched Mrs. Mallory open a bar of pink soap
from Sarah Dryden,
then a box of chocolates
from James Romano,
then a book
from Meredith Alvarez,
then a #1 TEACHER mug
from his best friend, Ajay,
then a long feather pen from Nicky Gregg.
No one had brought *anything* like Matt's good-bye present,
which was still in his backpack.

Mrs. Mallory dabbed her eyes with a handkerchief
when she read through the thank-you cards and notes.
She sniffled again when she snapped a photo
of each of her third graders.
Matt slicked his hair back
and smiled broadly when she took his picture.
He'd loved his year in Mrs. Mallory's class.

Then he remembered it was his last day as a third grader.
Next year he wouldn't be in Room 6.
He'd have a new group of classmates,
all fourth graders.
He'd be in a classroom far down the hall
and up the stairs,
on the second floor of Chapman Elementary School.
Cool.
Would his fourth grade teacher be Mrs. Quinn?
Or Mr. Bugliari?
Or Miss Burdett?

Time was running out.
Still, Matt wanted to wait and hand his teacher her gift
at the very end of the day.

Nobody else seemed to notice that the day
was a day to remember.
The whole school was too busy saying good-byes,
or having fun,
or celebrating,
or asking how next year
could ever match the one that had just gone by.

Then,
just as everyone in Room 6 was about to *explode*
with Last Day excitement,
the two room mothers arrived
with a big tray of ice-cream bars
and announced that Mr. Frazier had given permission
for a kickball game on the playground.
Mrs. Mallory's class lined up and headed outdoors.
Matt cheered for his winning team.
And he rounded the bases
with his usual lightning speed.

Of course,
that day Matt had still done his job
and made sure that Mrs. Mallory's clock
was keeping the right time.

Suddenly it was 2:20 P.M.
The 2:30 early-dismissal bell would be *bzzzzzz*ing soon!
Everyone checked inside their clean desks
for anything left behind
and zipped up their backpacks.

The countdown began again.
But now students were counting *minutes*
instead of days.

Ten . . .

nine . . .

eight . . .

seven . . .

six . . .

five . . .

four . . .

three . . .

two . . .

Matt pulled the wrapped gift from his backpack
and looked around the room for Mrs. Mallory.
He'd surprise her right after the bell rang.

"Time to get ready . . ."
"Time to go to your bus group . . ."
"I'll be thinking of all of you this summer!"
"And here's a good-bye hug for you . . .
and for you
and for you. . . ."
Matt heard his teacher's warm, familiar voice
above the final stacking of chairs upon desks in Room 6.
Then . . .

BZZZZZZZZZZZZZZZZZZZZZZZZZZZZZZ!

Throughout the Chapman classrooms and hallways
students and teachers clapped and cheered.

Yes!
School was out!
No more homework!
No more school lunches!
No more tests!
Tomorrow kids could sleep late!
Mrs. Mallory's class joined
in the pandemonium.

Lines of students dashed out of the school to their buses.
"Remember . . . no running in the halls. . . ."
The entire building echoed with voices.
Everyone was calling to friends:

"Good-bye . . . good-bye . . ."

"See you next fall!"

"Happy summer!"

Matt turned round and round,
scanning the classroom.
Where was his teacher?

Puzzled, he waited by her desk
as the rest of the class hurried out the door.
"Hey, where's Mrs. Mallory?" he asked.

"Bus duty!" Nicky yelled back.

Matt raced out of Room 6.
Dodging a slow line of kindergartners,
he ran down the crowded hall
with his present and his backpack.

Over the P.A. system
Mr. Frazier's calm voice
was announcing the bus dismissal.
"Bus 9 and Bus 14 are loading now . . . last call . . .
Bus 5 . . . walk to the right, please.
Have a great summer, everyone. . . ."

Bus 5 was Matt's bus.
Matt looked to the left
and then to the right.
Everywhere
dozens of students were in motion.

Where was Mrs. Mallory?

He had to say good-bye.
He had to say thank you.
He couldn't get on his bus—not yet.
The seconds were ticking by.

Matt stood outside the school building
in the warm sunshine,
holding his present under his arm.
He didn't even care
that the red-ribbon bow was crushed as flat as a pancake.

He saw Mrs. Bell in her SUMMER! T-shirt.
He saw Miss Knox, the music teacher,
talking to a parent.
He saw Mr. Fields directing bus traffic.
Where was Mrs. Mallory?

Matt blinked and felt a small flutter
of missing-a-good-friend panic.
He heard the engines of the remaining buses revving up
and saw students' faces at every window.
He heard Ajay
calling to him from their favorite seat,
telling Matt to hurry up.

Matt grabbed the present tightly
and sprinted toward Bus 5.

And then . . .
     there
         was
               Mrs. Mallory,
standing on the steps of his bus,
wildly waving her arms at him.

"Matthew Perez! Oh, Matt!
I've been *looking* for you!
I didn't get to say good-bye in the room
because I had to rush off to bus duty. . . .
I couldn't remember your bus number,
and I looked and looked on some other buses.
Then I finally remembered it was *Bus 5,*
but *you weren't on it!"*

Mrs. Mallory leaned down
and gave Matt a mother-hen hug.
"I wanted you to know
how much I am going to *miss* you next year!"

Matt sighed with relief.
"I've been looking for you, *too,*
Mrs. Mallory. . . .
I wanted to say good-bye too."

He handed the box to his teacher.
"Here's your present. . . .
I wanted to give it to you
the minute the dismissal bell rang.
I wrapped it in blue paper—for the *Cubs!*
It's smaller . . . but it keeps the right time."

And there,
with everyone on Bus 5 watching from their windows,
Mrs. Mallory opened the farewell gift
from her Official Timekeeper.
Overhead
a long stream of white cloud
moved slowly across the June sky.

Matt's teacher laughed out loud
and dabbed her eyes with her handkerchief
at the very same time.
And when Mrs. Mallory hugged him again,
she told Matthew Perez
it was the *best* last day of school
that she could ever remember.